Trains

Safe & Sound

By

Julie Chatton

Eloquent Books
New York, New York

Trains...Safe & Sound

Eloquent Books
An imprint of AEG Publishing Group
845 Third Avenue, 6th Floor - 6016
New York, NY 10022
www.eloquentbooks.com

ISBN: 978-1-60693-307-7
SKU: 1-60693-307-8

Printed in the United States of America

Book Design: Roger Hayes

Julie Chatton

Trains…

Safe & Sound

Curious???

Julie Chatton

Curious about trains???

TRAINS are much BIGGER than you can even imagine! If you've ever had the opportunity to go up close to a train, the size of it must have made you say to yourself "WOW." You may even say "WOW" out loud so everyone can hear. A train car can weigh more than 17 elephants. Trains are huge and very powerful. Once they start moving even ever so slightly, they are <u>not</u> easy to stop. You should never go near a train without an adult.

Julie Chatton

You must <u>always</u> and listen every time you get near a train track!

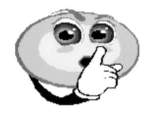

Trains are very loud. It is normal to think that no matter what you're doing you'd hear that train coming. But sometimes even a big loud train can sneak up on you.

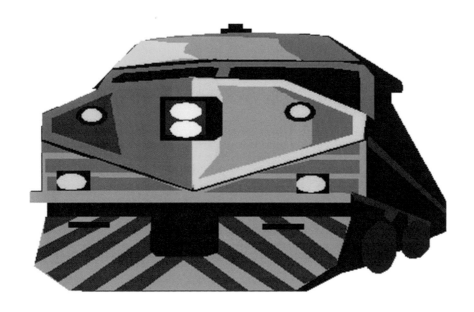

How can a train that big and that loud "sneak up" on you???

That is a Great question!!!

Think for a moment about the last time you rode in a car

or were on the school bus.

Can you remember everything that happened along the way? Did you arrive at school or home and think to yourself "I don't remember anything about the ride, we got here so fast."

Some times while you're awake and walking and talking, it seems that you can be far-far away in your thoughts.

You may not even realize it, but you are thinking of other things that keep your mind so busy that all sorts of noises are taking place all around you but you don't even notice. It is during those moments of time that you may not even hear a train.

If you are becoming curious about trains or the train tracks, do not try to go and see for yourself or even with a group of friends. Always talk to an adult. They can help answer your questions.

If you want to get a better look at a real train, ask your mom or dad to take you on a train ride or to sit with them and watch the trains go by from a safe spot far enough away.

Understand that you need to stay safe around trains, <u>all the time</u>.

Freight trains are used to transport goods or materials like toys and books. Fuel to heat our homes may travel by train. A freight train is basically a train that does not carry passengers. Transporting products by freight train saves energy when the freight is being carried in large quantities and over long distances. There are more freight trains on the United States train tracks than passenger trains.

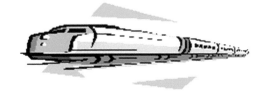

Passenger trains are called commuter trains. These trains travel from station to station in the cities and suburban neighborhoods to help people get from place to place. Trains are necessary in the world today.

Some people take the train to work instead of driving a car.

Some people take the train to go on vacation.

It is a very safe way to travel.

For many people their job is to work on a train.

The Engineer is the driver.

The Conductor will take your ticket and will help you on and off the train. (It is a very big step)

14

Some people live in homes near the train tracks. The houses are always built a safe distance away.

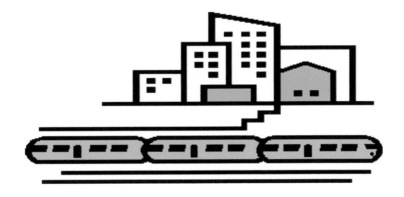

Trains go all over the country. It's hard to avoid having houses near them. The people who live near the train know that every day they need to be careful if they are by the tracks. If they are not careful, they can get hurt.

At the place where the train crosses over a street or sidewalk, there is usually a signal of lights, bells and/or a gate that comes down, warning of an approaching train.

It makes a loud sound and blocks the train tracks so no one can cross over to the other side. Everyone should stop and wait. When the train is gone, the bells and lights turn off and the gates open so you can approach and get to the other side if you need to.

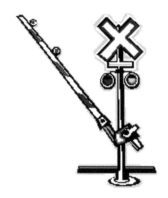

The train tracks go for miles and miles before and after the places which signal warning. Sometimes a curious person may wonder what it's like on those tracks.

Well it's not the place to be or play that's for sure!

Without the signal to let you know of a train approaching, a train can come up at anytime and surprise you.

You may think that it's not possible to surprise you because they are so big and loud, but it can happen.

Another danger about playing around the train tracks is that people can get hurt even though they know they need to get away.

They can see and hear the train but they can't get off the tracks in time because their shoelace or foot or their hand or jacket gets caught in the tracks.

When this happens they panic because they are trying so hard to get away. The train Engineer sees the person trying to get away and he tries to stop, but he can't just stop the train, it's too big and moves too fast.

Usually when this happens someone gets hurt and maybe

they die. Everyone is scared and sad when this happens because it should never have happened. People are <u>not</u> supposed to be on the tracks!!!

Sometimes adults get impatient when they are in a hurry.

They see a train sitting in the station. If the gates are down they are not supposed to cross the tracks, but some people decide to drive around the gates anyway. This is a really bad idea because even though they see a train sitting in the station, there may be another train passing through on the next track that they can not see. This is always a bad situation.

If the gates are down then no one should cross!

Sometimes the gates are not working right. It may be that the gates are down even though there is not a train in the area. When this happens,

a police officer will check out the problem and direct traffic to get you across safely while the problem is being fixed.

Most train accidents can be avoided if <u>everyone</u> always thinks about safety.

Remember trains can be fascinating to look at and wonderful for transportation, but they can be very dangerous.

Julie Chatton

When you are near a train or train tracks,

<u>REMEMBER TO ALWAYS BE AWARE!</u>

Look… Listen… and Live!

23

LaVergne, TN USA
21 December 2009
167728LV00002B